Small Rabbit

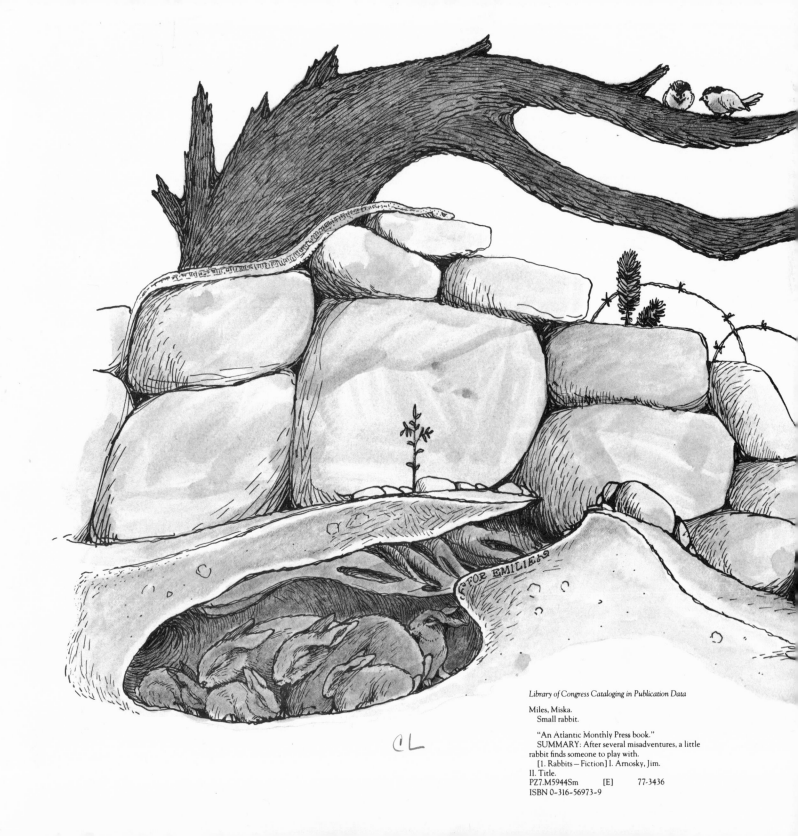

FOR EMILIE

Library of Congress Cataloging in Publication Data

Miles, Miska.
  Small rabbit.

  "An Atlantic Monthly Press book."
  SUMMARY: After several misadventures, a little
rabbit finds someone to play with.
  [1. Rabbits — Fiction] I. Arnosky, Jim.
II. Title.
PZ7.M5944Sm   [E]   77-3436
ISBN 0-316-56973-9

Small Rabbit

by

Miska Miles

Illustrated by

Jim Arnosky

An Atlantic Monthly Press Book

Little, Brown and Company

Boston   Toronto

Small rabbit kicked out at her father.

"Let's go out and play," she said.

"Suppose YOU go out and play," her father said.

The mother rabbit twitched her whiskers.

"Suppose you go outside and find a friend to play with."

"And then you can come back
and tell us all about it," the father
rabbit said.

"There are things to watch for,"
the mother rabbit said. "Enemies.
Hawk. Fox. Human."

"How will I know when I see a
hawk?" the small rabbit asked.

"The hawk soars through the sky,"
her father said. "And when he sees
you, he will swoop down—if you see
a hawk, RUN."

"I'll run."

Small rabbit flicked one ear.

"How will I know when I see a fox?" she said.

"He has a pointed nose," the mother rabbit said. "And he'll creep through the bushes to catch you."

Small rabbit shivered.

"And the human stands on two legs," the father rabbit said. "Humans want everything they see."

"If you see a hawk or a fox or a human, you RUN," the mother rabbit said. "Running is what you do best."

"How will I know when I find a friend?" the small rabbit asked.
"You'll know," the father said.

"And watch out for bushes with burrs," the mother rabbit said. "Burrs get caught in your fur."

Alone, the small rabbit hopped outside.

She sniffed.

A soft breeze parted her fur.

She hopped along—watching—watching—and on she went through the grass.

She came to a field of white daisies
and red clover.

She wriggled her nose and started
to eat.

Two butterflies swooped above her head.

"HAWKS!"

Small rabbit flashed away through the daisies.

She slid into a ditch and crouched there.

Her heart fluttered against her ribs.

And when the butterflies were gone, she crept out, hopping here and hopping there, nibbling at green leaves of chicory and bugle weed.

A sharp-nosed creature came dart-
ing through the weeds.

"A FOX!"

Small rabbit dashed away.

She found a small hole where
Queen Anne's lace grew tall, and
she hunched there, listening—

When at last she dared to go out,
she hopped along, turning her ears
to listen. The sun shone and she
hopped high because the day was so
beautiful and she was so brave.

In the shadow of a rock, she saw a fat, lumpy creature.

"Are you a friend?" the small rabbit asked.

The toad flicked out his tongue, caught a fly, and closed his eyes.

Small rabbit went on past the rock.
From a hole on the crest of a small
hill, a flat face looked out at her.

"Are you a friend?" the small
rabbit asked.

The woodchuck was gone, back
into his burrow.
The small rabbit went on.

When she came to a patch of hard
dirt under an oak tree, she saw a fear-
some thing.

The thing lifted himself high on
his back feet, an acorn between his
two front paws.

"TWO LEGS," the small rabbit
said.

"A HUMAN."

Like lightning she ran toward a
tangle of bramble bushes.
She shoved into them.
Something was following her.

She turned and saw a furry face
and bright, brown eyes.

"Did you see the human?" the
small rabbit asked.

"No," said the stranger. "I saw you
run, so I ran, too."

Small rabbit and the stranger
huddled side by side.

And when they could see no
danger and hear no danger, they
wiggled themselves free from the
bushes.

Small rabbit stopped suddenly.
She lifted a paw.

"A burr," said the stranger. "It's
caught between the pads of your toes.
I can help." He took the burr between his teeth. He tugged.

Out it came with a little tuft of
fur.

"Want to come for supper?" the
small rabbit asked. "My mother won't
care."

"I don't mind," the stranger said.

Slowly the small rabbit led the way
home.

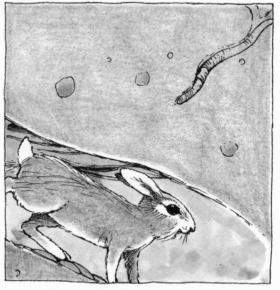

They plopped down inside the burrow.

"I'M HOME," the small rabbit said.

"Good," said her father.

"I had a big day," she said. "I saw two hawks and a fox."

"NO!" said her father.

"And I saw a human."
"NO!" said her mother.

"And I got a burr in my paw and
my friend helped me. Now I know
everything a rabbit needs to know.
And I found a friend. He came for
supper. Can he stay?"

"He can stay," the mother rabbit said.

So they all went outside for supper—the small rabbit, her family and her friend.

Books by Miska Miles